AMAZONIKA
AND THE MAJESTIC FIGHT
FOR THE ORBS OF LIFE

AMAZONIKA AND THE MAJESTIC FIGHT FOR THE ORBS OF LIFE

By Donna Anita Bennett

CONTENTS

ACKNOWLEDGEMENT

I dedicate this book to a woman named Hazel, whose spirit was as bright as the sun. She was a beacon of light that shined on so many people throughout her life. She had her share of struggles, but her biggest fight left her helpless, weak, and tired. So, as a badge of honor, she wore her smile so proudly throughout her pain. Her smile was contagious whenever she entered a room. And her laughter would allow you to join right in without even knowing what made her laugh.

Life chose her, and she gave life to five beautiful daughters and a handsome son. She was a special lady who had high standards, and as a strong woman, she raised her children the best way she knew how. Thank you for the strength, love, wisdom, and values you courageously taught us. Thank you so much, Mom, for choosing me as one of your beautiful daughters. And through it all, you taught us how to live, love, and laugh. And as our mother, you wouldn't have us live our lives any other way.

Mom, I remember the day you said to me, "When you can find love in your heart, it becomes the most important thing in your life. It makes everything else seem less important. So learn to love yourself first, and embrace the fact that all of you look different, and you are different because each one of you have your mother's love. That's what makes you all a driving force in my life as your mother, to have chosen you all as my children."

Then with a whisper, she said, "I love everyone of you."

PREFACE

"If you could live your life over again, would you change a thing?" Allow me to repeat that: "If I could live my life all over again, yes, I would change some things."

What is life as we see it? My thoughts are it's nothing more than existence with a purpose, which has the tendency to assist you in living a much better life. It can make all the difference in the world when you make a decision to stick to something in order to develop a passion or desire.

My son convinced me to buy a new computer chair to move forward in my passion to write, so I did. The new chair, although a bit pricey, gave me the means and support I needed to focus on completing and achieving my passion in writing my first book. I want to thank my son, Micah, my daughter, April, and my son-in-law, Rodney, for all their wonderful support. As I touch my heart and take a bow, thank you!

For reasons I cannot quite explain, when something comes to me, I write it down and then I find myself creating a poem or a gifted letter to give to family or friends. But I never thought to just sit down to see what I could do as far as staying true to something that really had my interest.

So in light of it all, I feel so encouraged now to continue this project to maybe write a second story about the orbs in waterfall bay, knowing that it will give me a stronger sense of confidence as I develop the ability to become one of the best writers. Just messing with you-we'll see.

I hope that as you read on you will enjoy the findings.

INTRODUCTION

So I embraced an idea to write about Amazonika a fictional rain forest that was created as a paradise. And a water lily that was looked upon as a mother figure of all who resides in the rain forest. Hazel was her name and being of sound mind, and having a strong constitution as a human being, she mastered the ability to transform herself into a big water lily. As she lived her secret life in the rain forest. And as a water lily she learned how to survive, as a beautiful plant; that had the responsibilities for keeping a clear and clean-looking pond, in a place she stumble into and called Waterfall Bay.

Hazel who is a strong character in this book, has another entity namely, Unee as a human force, that comes alive. She is a water lily and a human, both having intriguing characters that press upon love, and values. Along with her other amazing powers, she represented a loving mother that was dear to my heart.

Having a love for butterflies and their many species, Hazel has to comes to terms in confronting: a lost Queen Alexandra bird wing butterfly, named Maya who wants to take on the human form of a little girl; who has an amazing spirit as she finds love, family, and friends to add to her own family that she thought she lost but later were found.

And Lezah who was a smart, and loving little girl from a town called Rambling Woods, who is trying to find her way in a new town, and how she slips inside an open fictional book into another dimension and finds her lost grandmother, and makes many new friends throughout her journey. It also shares her enriched finding, and her enlightenment of knowing that she also has special powers and gifts.

Lezah's mother, Zora, in the story, finds herself in a place she never thought existed, when she discovers the library book found by her daughter and what lies inside. Zora finds an opening as she reads the library book and disappears into an imaginary paradise, a window to her daughter's disappearance and into a strange new world. As she exit out of her real life into an extraordinary life of the Amazonika rain forest in Waterfall Bay.

Finally, they all encounter their own unique abilities as changes are made in their lives. As war takes place, in the rain forest they must find a way to protect themselves and the fate of a new world that is coming. As they face distractions made by Jubu, an evil tyrant and shape-shifter who set out to take the orbs from the cities and their planets, leaving them helpless and weak without life support. The orbs are the greatest power sources for their planets.

In every good there is some bad, and for every problem there is always a solution.

Without further ado, let's begin.

1

THE MYSTERIOUS LIBRARY BOOK

As the large moving van pulled up to park right in front of 3719 Spider Webb Drive, the front door opened wide from inside. Lezah couldn't wait for the van to arrive. She was on her way out the door to explore the new neighborhood, wearing her sassy blue jeans while tying her kente cloth scarf around her head as a hair band. She shouted, "Mom, the movers are here."

Her mom, Zora Hany, stepped away from the boxes to go outside and see for herself. She then made it clear by saying to her daughter, Lezah, "Be careful and be sure to take your key." Ever since she was six years old, Lezah had been a latchkey child. She was now coming of age and would be ten in a few months. Lezah and her mom had a great relationship that came first and foremost. Their relationship had its share of discipline, which was maintained and very much understood.

Secondly, they worked together in being each other's best friends. Lezah was young when her grandmother on her mother's side of the family disappeared.

It was believed that her grandmother had some deep dark secrets. There were hushed rumors.

Truth be told, her grandmother was thought to be clairvoyant, claiming to have shown some abilities of supernatural gifts to perceive events in

the future or beyond normal sensory contact. It was mentioned that she had inherited a wide range of abilities as well as being gifted. There were not many conversations about her after her disappearance.

Lezah's father had worked for a construction company. He was a builder, who had an unfortunate accident and died instantly a few years before Lezah and her mother moved to Rambling Woods.

Lezah knew her father and grandmother very well. Even as a child, she inherited some similarities from both, and she loved and missed them very much. Even to this day, she missed their love the most. Now, Lezah's mom from day one taught her to be very responsible. For a while now, it had been the two of them, ever since her father passed away and her grandmother disappeared. As a single parent now, Zora works hard, taking overtime work on the weekends.

Lezah was an only child, who has learned to embrace the love of life and family. They moved from a small town in Richmond to a place called Rambling Woods in a quiet but friendly neighborhood.

One thing was for sure: it felt like a wonderful place where everybody welcomed them with open arms. Along with making them feel welcome, the neighbors' warm smiles made a brighter light that got them through their unpacking with ease.

In this quiet but friendly neighborhood, Lezah and her mother believed one thing for sure: that everyone here had love in their hearts. Lezah's mom didn't have to cook for a few days because their neighbors came over with casserole dishes and baked goods for delicious meals.

All kinds of tasty aromas of delightful menus with familiar flavors permeated throughout the house. It was like a Thanksgiving feast to enjoy.That first night, after saying grace and enjoying a wonderful meal, Lezah's mom said to her daughter, "We are so blessed to have found such wonderful neighbors. They are caring and loving people. I'm sure your father would have approved and he would have loved to be here as well."

Lezah was looking forward to making new friends. She walked to school and studied hard to stay on top of her skills. One day after school, she took a walk further into town and spotted an old-fashioned library.

She went inside to speak with the librarian to see if she could find adventure, science fiction, or time travel books.

As she approached the librarian, she said, "Hello, I'm interested in finding some adventure stories."

"Follow me," said, the librarian, as they both headed toward the back of the library to check. "Here you will find most of the books you are looking for. Please let me know if you are looking for a specific book. Just give me the title and the author." "I may have to place an order for you if we don't carry it here at this library." The librarian then asked, "Do you have a library card with us?"

Lezah said, "I just moved here a few weeks ago."

"Is there a form I can fill out?"

"Sure," said, the librarian. "You need some form of identification." Lezah presented her school ID, which showed her photo and school name.

"We are all set," said the librarian. So after that was completed, Lezah decided to browse through some books in the back. Moving toward the front, she saw a book in the window that got her attention. She couldn't find anything she thought would be more interesting than that book in the window. So she approached the librarian for a request to take out the book, hoping that it would be available.

"May I please see that book in the window?" she asked.

"Oh, that book," the librarian said. "That's a special book. That book has more adventures than any other books you have ever read."

"Here, take a look."

Lezah opened the book, but there were no words. As the librarian was about to walk away, Lezah asked softly, "Wait, what is this?"

The librarian responded, "The words in this book are hidden, and in order to reveal them, your heart must be in the right place."

"My heart is in the right place," said Lezah.

"Then the book is yours. Here, take this book," said the librarian.

"Please promise to take good care of this book. It's old, and it has a lot of wear and tear.

It has passed through the lives of many readers, who have time traveled through these pages. It must be returned in three weeks."

After filling out a form for a library card, Lezah checked out the book and carefully put it in her backpack. As she was leaving the library, she couldn't wait to get home to open the book.

Not having walked a half a block, she looked back at the old-fashioned library, but to her surprise, it had vanished. She walked back to make sure, and it was not there. How could this be? she thought.

That was strange, so she took her backpack off to see if the book was still in her backpack. Sure enough, it was still there. Lezah was not aware that, by reading this book, it would lead her to the whereabouts of her grandmother.

When Lezah got home, her mom was still at work. She grabbed a snack, and with excitement she ventured upstairs to her room and removed the book from her backpack. When she opened the book, there were only blank pages. She closed it again and then touched the picture of the large water lily on the cover. There was a shimmer from the painting, a glow that meant something.

She proceeded to open the book again. All the words started to appear, and she began to read.

"Life is amazing and exciting. As we all know, the sun has the most incredible task. Flying way up in the sky is a tireless butterfly that continue to travel among the swarm of butterflies. This butterfly has been flying in the wrong direction for several hours. And she was larger than other butterflies. She spotted a pond that was big. It was huge. While she was flying and looking down below with no idea, she landed on a water lily.

"Oh my," said the water lily. "Who gave you the right to rest on me?"

"Oops," said the butterfly. "I'm sorry this pond is so big. As you can see, I thought I would have enough room to allow me to rest here."

"I can see that," said the water lily, "but you have landed on some of me instead of on my pond."

"Anyway, who gave you permission to land here period?"

"No one," said the butterfly. "No one." "I have been flying for hours and got lost. I thought it would be okay to rest here for a while."

But the water lily was so big and shouted, "Just because you can fly and can see from up there doesn't give you the right to land on my lily pad in my pond."

Again, the butterfly said, "I'm so sorry."

As Lezah continued to read, she took a deep breath and thought for a minute. A real, live, talking water lily. What an adventure, she thought. And that poor butterfly.

Lezah closed her eyes, and with her strong imagination, something happened. She found herself present in the midst of the water lily and butterfly's ordeal. She tried to stay hidden among the greens in the rain forest; she couldn't help herself. She continued to hear both the water lily and butterfly in a boisterous confrontation.

2

INSIDE AMAZONIKA

"**A**m I being interrupted?" asked the water lily. "Who dares to be present and does not announce who they are?" Again, the water lily paused as she thought she'd heard something. "Who's there?" "Who's there?"

Before the butterfly could answer, the water lily heard noises coming from the bushes not far away. "Show yourself." "Come out, whoever you are, and reveal yourself. Please let us know who you are and what you are doing out there among those bushes."

The little girl came out smiling. She had never seen anything so beautiful. There was an unusual sense of love surrounding the entire rain forest.

"My child, wherever did you come from and how did you get here?" "You are not from around here. What do they call you? Are you lost?"

She walked toward the water lily and said, "My name is Lezah, and I'm nine years old, soon to be ten in a few months." "I don't think I'm lost. I was reading a book, and as if by magic, I somehow got here."

"You must be from the earth's realm," said the water lily.

"Yes, ma'am," she answered.

"Well, can you get back?" asked the water lily.

"I'm not sure," said Lezah with a smile.

The water lily looked at the butterfly, who continued to say she was sorry, and asked, "What is your name?"

The frightened butterfly quickly said, "My name is Maya."

The water lily then made an announcement: "My children, my name is Hazel. I am a water lily, and both of you have landed in my rain forest." For a moment Hazel felt a need to hug Maya. As she was crying, her tears were so painful, with more than enough sadness for one individual to have to endure.

As Lezah looked on, as all eyes were now on her, she asked, "May I please say something, Miss Hazel?" "I realized that I got here through some kind of teleportation I believe that as a dictionary meaning, teleportation is the theoretical transfer of matter or energy from one point to another without traversing the physical space between them."

"What I'm trying to explain in plain English is that I got here by closing my eyes and taking a deep breath. I then imagined that if I could get into this story, I would find some adventure." "Well anyway, Miss Hazel, who needs a magic carpet if you can teleport yourself and your belongings from one place to another yourself?" Lezah laughed as she realized that she was talking too much. "Oops!" she went on further to say. "I guess that was to much unnecessary information."

"Well perhaps you can come closer and tell me more," said Hazel.

Lezah came forward, and while Hazel was trying to reason with Maya to stop crying, Lezah started to develop teary eyes as well. She decided to get closer to Maya so she could whisper, "Maya, don't cry. You're a big beautiful butterfly. I'll be your friend."

"Okay," said Maya, "friends."

"Listen Maya," said Lezah. "Maybe you can speak with Miss Hazel. I'm sure she will help you and guide you back if you think you are lost."

"Here, you can wipe your tears away."

Lezah reached in back of her head and untied her kente cloth scarf used to hold back her beautiful soft locks of hair. "You see," my scarf has many colors: black for maturation that intensified spiritual energy; maroon the color of Mother Earth associated with healing; blue for peaceful harmony and love; green for the vegetation, planting harvesting, growth, and spiritual renewal; and gold for royalty, wealth, high status, glory, and spiritual purity."

Lezah presented Maya with her beautiful scarf so that her tears could prove to become a part of her family if nothing else. Since birth Lezah has always wore kente cloth fabrics; it represents her people of color.

As Maya quieted down, she began to tell Miss Hazel her story. In a soft voice, she described the war between the kaleidoscope, insects, butterflies, moths, and other creatures of the air great and small. She got turned around, and before she knew it, she got lost. And that was how she landed in Hazel's pond.

"I wished, Miss Hazel, that I was a child instead of a butterfly," Maya said, "so I could have strong legs to laugh, run, play, and learn. What I really want is to be knowledgeable in a way that could help." "Becoming human has always been my ultimate secret wish."

Maya started to cry even harder, with tears flowing down her big butterfly cheeks into the pond. "I have a brother, you know. His name is Adonis," said Maya, "and we shared a lot together. Our father got lost in the war, and our mother was always working and helping others. So we had to care for each other. I don't know where to find my brother."

"Maya, we will find him," Hazel said.

She continued to assure Maya that everything would work out fine, and she would ask for the help of everyone she knew in and around the pond. Things got started after Maya shared her story. It was a beginning to search. It would allow some time to find the means to an end of what has been taking place. And it would create more awareness for Hazel to understand more of what was going on in Maya's life.

"Come closer, my child. Life is so unpredictable for reasons only God and the universe understand," Hazel said. "We must learn to make the best of everything at all times and love ourselves first and foremost before we can show love to others. Maya, I want you to meet Mr. Sun." Suddenly a beautiful beam became radiant to the eyes of Maya and Lezah.

It was the brightest light they both had ever seen. Mr. Sun approved of Maya and Lezah as friends. While Lezah looked on, she kept quiet so not to cause any disturbance.

Maya looked at Lezah and whispered, "I'm so glad to have you as a friend."

Hazel introduced them to the rippling waters, trees and foliage, and the pool of fish; the beautiful bright flowers and the greens all around the pond; the waterfalls and so much beyond their wildest dreams; and lastly the soft whispers of the breeze.

Now Hazel shared with them a little something about herself. "I tend to grow in clusters, which can even sometimes cover the surface of my pond. With leaves and petals, this helps to block too much sunlight and keep the temperature of my pond low in the summertime.

As a water lily, I provide shelter for fish who need a short period of rest or relief from the sunlight or who are hiding from predators.

"As a plant that blooms from June to September, my plant life serves me well. I open in the morning to catch the sunlight, while closing in the late afternoon or evening gives me the much-needed rest and longevity.

I have been told that my fragrance is fresh and lightly sweet a little aquatic with a touch of lemon. I'm unforgettable as a lily even though I go dormant during the winter; I must be careful not to freeze, because I would die."

"Have you ever thought about becoming something other than a water lily?" asked Maya.

"Why, yes," said Hazel. "First, please allow me to say this: "I know who I am, and I know where I'm going. I would consider myself a wise water lily, who has learned much during her time.

I'm looked upon as a mother figure. All the fishes, birds, trees and all other flying creatures in the air and on land seek me out for guidance and advice. I can always learn from the smallest whispers of the winds and the rippling waters. Even the rain tells me a story, and the sun has always brightened my way. I have become who I wanted to be: a strong, wise, loving and grateful water lily."

Hazel then asked, "Maya, did you ever wonder what it would be like to take on a human form?"

3

AMAZONIKA THE RAIN FOREST

"What kind of human did you want to become?" asked Hazel. "A girl the same age as Lezah." said Maya.

So Hazel worked her magic, and all the beautiful butterflies from all corners of the sky started to reappear, forming an image of a human hand at first, working their way up the arms. Then, suddenly, the butterflies were so excited that, with an outburst of laughter, the image disappeared. And all the butterflies disappeared. And the thought creating the child image evaporated in an instant.

"Well," said Hazel, "you have a lot to learn, Maya."

"Hazel said that Maya would have another chance to become a child." "In the meantime, first things first. Knowledge is the forbidden fruit, and time will tell as you begin to learn."

Suddenly, right before Hazel's eyes there was a beautiful transformation.

Seahorses, dolphins, mermaids, and beautiful colored fish all gathered around and formed something awesome:

a human, a blue print of a child, a sketch so bright that it had the attention of all those who were around. They were astonished by what they saw in this creation of humanity.

A child's hand, arm, and shoulder were formed to be the unique image of Maya's deepest wish. But as quickly as it appeared, that's how fast it vanished. The brightness faded, and in an instant, everything collapsed. Yet it was so real for the other creatures in and around the pond, who were somewhat more sincere. Again, Hazel confirmed that there was a lot for Maya to do and to learn before miracles could take hold.

Everyone could see, though, that Maya was special, and Hazel would have to teach her the values and principle of life and the art of the other species. Lezah paused for a minute as her ears picked up signals. She blinked really hard as she heard her mother calling her to come down for dinner. After closing her eyes, she was back in her bedroom.

Lezah had no idea that next time would be her last time to return back home. She was about to take on the ultimate time travel; there would be no possible way for her to return back to earth.

Although she could not afford to disappear now that her mother was at home, she gathered all her books and homework assignments to do downstairs after she finished her dinner.

Lezah was smart to do this, as it would give her time to converse with her mom and not allow her to be suspicious. She didn't want her mom to know anything about the book she got from the library.

Maybe I can find some time after dinner when my homework is finished to go back to reading the book, Lezah thought. So she put the book back under her bed.

When it was time for Lezah to turn in for the night, she kept falling in and out of sleep as she waited patiently for her mother to settle down and turn the lights out.
Lezah knew that her mom enjoyed taking a tranquil bath after dinner to help her relax after putting in a hard day at work. Zora worked in a hospital as a nurse; at times she found it very exhausting.

She would always fall asleep in the tub, and it would take Lezah's knock on the bathroom door having to use the bathroom to wake her mom.

Lezah found herself getting antsy and restless waiting to get back to reading the book, still hidden underneath her bed. For hours after her bathroom visit, she couldn't get to sleep, and before too long the morning had arrived. Because morning was waiting around the corner, Lezah managed to fall fast asleep.

In the morning, Lezah knew she couldn't start something that would be difficult to finish and had no choice but to wait until after school. Plus, Zora always made time for them to have morning breakfast smoothies, home fries, and homemade French toast. Lezah's mother worked the early shift and had been on day shift for a while now. She put in a lot of overtime on the weekends. It had been hard for her since her husband passed away, but she always made the best of all things in sharing with her daughter Lezah.

A day never went by without her mother saying to her, "We're going to be just fine, because we have each other."

Lezah's day at school was good although she still had'nt met any true friends that she would feel comfortable sharing secrets with. Walking home, she was intrigued by thoughts of opening that book from the library.

As she approached her house, she reached for the chain around her neck to get her key and opened the front door. She always made sure that when she got inside the house, the door was locked and secured before doing anything else.

The phone rang right on time. Her mother would always check on Lezah after school to make sure she was okay. Knowing that Lezah had reached home safe and sound would always allow her to feel better about her daughter being alone.

But this time Zora's call was to tell her daughter, Lezah, that she had to work a bit late, because her coworker who was to replace her shift was running late, and she would be staying at the hospital for no more than a few hours. On that note, Lezah felt that it was a good time to get back to her book. She poured herself a glass of milk with a chocolate cookie and went upstairs to her room.

She placed the glass on her nightstand, and while still eating her cookie, she placed the book on her bed to continue the story. "Let's see now," she said. "Oh! Right here is where I stopped." And so she read.

"Maya the butterfly took a look into the water and saw herself for the first time. There were no colors, not even a hue that would appear beautiful as a butterfly. When she looked down into the pond, she realized that she was an ordinary plain butterfly without a personality. Maya had never seen herself, not even in a mirror, and she had no idea that her appearance was something of beauty. All she saw was a big, frightened butterfly.

Then again, she was never told that she was from the family line of Queen Alexandra bird wings, who are large and beautiful.

As she peered in the water, right beside her stood a baby deer, a doe and a buck. They resembled each other as a family with a mother, father, and baby. Maya began to weep as she thought about her mother, father, and brother. And the disappointment she found in herself was now an open book. Every tear that dropped into the pond would create an image of someone she lost or missed in her life.

Lezah feels her pain as she reads on. Now as Maya tried hard to visualize and make light of the images, the baby deer approached her with a smile.

"Hello," said the deer. "Where is your mother?"

Maya teared up, saying, "I don't know."

"Why don't you know?" asked the baby deer. That was all she needed to hear to give way to endless weeping.

Hazel was giving Maya some time alone when she heard her weeping, so she came over to calm her down. Maya let go of her tears and Hazel proceeded to share a story about a bit of what life is all about. "There is always a lot of sunshine here in the rain forest.

When it gets too cold, it allows me to position myself where there is still a breath of sunlight or until the warm weather returns. Although as I look further down, there is a stream of slowly moving water with floating leaves with beautiful round lily pads and frogs resting on them."

"For now, this is my home, and this is where I'm supposed to be with all its thick underwater stems buried in the mud and the long stalks reaching up from the stem to support me." "I believe in the universe, Maya, said Hazel, and that has a lot to do with your happiness and whether you remain a butterfly or become worthy of transformation."

4

MISS HAZEL,
LEZAH, MAYA, AND FRIENDS

"I believe also in a higher power that has created us all and that we can pray to for guidance," Hazel continued. "Things just don't happen. There is a reason for everything that transpires in our lives." "Maya, what is your vision in life, and why are you here?' I know that you are lost; however, before this happened, who really is Maya? What is her vision or quest in life?" "I really don't know, Miss Hazel. Please help me to solve those questions in my life so that I can propose a better one."

Hazel whispered softly, "I will, Maya, I will."

Now, as Lezah continued to read and listen at the same time, she found the conversation with Maya and Miss Hazel very touching. She didn't realize her tears fell onto the page, and like magic again, it took her right into the story. Spontaneously, by closing her eyes and at the same time releasing her tears, she was now in the rain forest. She heard Hazel's voice. "Is that you, Lezah?" "Why are you in and out of the rain forest?" "Are you in need of help?" Lezah answered, "I want to be your student."

And so Hazel proceeded. "Life is a convention, and everyone is caught up into one big shindig. Mind you, everyone wants to have the floor and speak, yet no one is listening. For now, let's make it a point to listen as we go along and then we all can learn from each other. I know you want to take on a human form, Maya. But why?"

Maya spoke very clearly. "I want the characteristics of a human body with a soul, to be distinguished from an animal or other insects."

"It would be a miracle if it were possible, but as a butterfly, I find that I am limited," Maya said. "I'm a winged creature who is invisible, who cannot find her real colors to allow everyone to see her abilities. I can only pollinate, which makes me less than unique. I have four stages: first as an egg; next a caterpillar, which is called the larva; then a pupa, which is when the caterpillar is done growing; and lastly the butterfly comes out. The thing about butterflies is that they have a short life expectancy."

"I can still remember when my wings were damp and soft and were folded against my body. I could not fly. I had to pump the blood into my wings, so I had to get them working and flapping."

"After I did that, I was able to learn how to fly. I couldn't fly well at first; I needed a lot of practice and it didn't take me long before I knew how to fly really fast. The first thing you do when you learn how to fly is to look for food. As I get older, I'm sure it will become time for me to find a mate. I just don't want my life as a butterfly to become more unreal than what it is without longevity and family. Right now, I have no one. My life should be exciting, but it hasn't been for a while."

So now, both Hazel and Maya paused to try to figure it all out. Then Hazel gave it some thought. Life is not always normal. In fact life can't possibly be normal, because everything changes and nothing ever remains the same. It just makes things complicated, I guess, as this gives me a sense of where we are going as of right now, being that we are in a state of war all around us.

"I believe that a human war is the most devastating kind of battle. It seems that all kinds of animals and insects of the earth have a form of armor that is used to protect themselves from the devastation they cause to one another. I must say we all die out in every species in life, truth be told."

"So now that we both know a little bit more about each other," Hazel said, "let's begin our journey. We need to find your parents and your brother. Themba, who is our head of military here, will be assigned the task to find your parents. She is an African bald eagle. She was given that name, because she is large in size and holds values of trust, hope, and strong faith, as she accomplishes every assignment with honors."

"Themba governs the skies in a way that no one else can or ever will. We all are so lucky to have her. She was once lost and broken and has found her place here, where she was healed and mended. Now she has settled her differences to begin anew. Just because life hands you disappointments doesn't give you the right to let go. Hold on tight, and see where it will take you. Go ahead. Move in other areas to become the best you can be on your terms, and follow your dreams."

"Try learning to say, "I am who I am, because I am stronger than you think I am, and I will not allow anyone or anything to break me down or deny who I am and settle for failure."

"And you, Lezah," said Hazel, "what are your dreams, visions, and spirations in life, now that you are one of my students? I welcome all those who want knowledge." "Because if I teach you something that you already know, then you have not learned anything." "So, speak up, Lezah."

"Miss Hazel, I'm here because I want to learn as much as I can. And if Themba can help Maya, then maybe my grandmother can be found as well."

"Okay," said, Hazel, "I see and understand why we always have to wear our boxing gloves and awake each day prepared for a fight for life." "Tell me, my dear," "how long has your grandmother been missing, and what world has she vanished from?"

"Oh, that's right, Lezah, you are from the earth's realm." Always keep things real; never make things personal. That's when it became a struggle in trying to please everybody all the time.

"Stop allowing people, places, and things that happen in your life to cause you to say it's a struggle and you cannot make it. Stop and take a minute to look down the road ahead of you, place your shoes on your feet, and walk your way into finding the things that will enhance and build your life.

Don't allow any of the people, places, and things you meet along the way make or break your concentration in life. It will only happen if you allow that to happen."

Hazel made it her duty to assist Lezah in finding her grandmother as well. Lezah continued to listen, not permitting herself to be distracted by any thoughts of Rambling Woods. She was now on a mission to find her grandmother. It was all about learning all she could and staying in the present at Waterfall Bay.

Slipping away over the waterfall, darkness descended upon the rain forest and everyone was getting sleepy. There was a small cave hidden under a ledge with rocks, large leaves, and some palm tree branches placed together inside to form a sleeping area for Lezah and the others. It was put together by the animals of the rain forest.

It also had a table created out of rocks and stones. On the table was a large bowl with fresh fruits and veggies. Lezah saw her sleeping area and managed to lie down and fall fast asleep. She was very tired.

Then Maya found her way over to the end of the sleeping area creating a makeshift blanket for Lezah with her wings to keep her warm throughout the night.

When Zora got home, it was late. She was so tired that she went straight to bed. As morning approached, she got up to check on Lezah, and saw that her bed had been made, and she was gone. This is strange, she thought. Why would she leave the house so early without breakfast or saying good-bye? She got worried and even felt a little guilty. No overtime for me tonight. She would come home early to prepare Lezah's favorite dish and stop by the bakery along the way and pick up some sweets. She wanted to be home before her daughter to give her a big surprise.

Morning came with a beautiful sunrise, and looking out of the cave you could see the sun rising as bright as can be. Lezah sat up and stretched her arms straight up to the heavens.

She yawned and immediately remembered that she was still in the tropical rain forest. She saw a panther asleep in the corner of the cave. She also realized that Maya's wings had kept her warm throughout the night. As she stood up, Maya fluttered her wings to get up as well.

"I had an awesome night, and I had the best sleep ever," Lezah said. "What about you Maya?"

"I did too, Lezah. It was wonderful," the butterfly said.

Lezah and Maya went outside to get closer to the pond where they saw Hazel, and they both wished her good morning together in one voice.

"Good morning." Hazel said. "I hope Zephaniah didn't frighten you two. He's harmless. His name means "God has hidden." Hazel called out to Zephaniah the panther. "Come out to meet some new friends."

Out came Zephaniah so calm, relaxed, and happy. He took a minute to stretch before he approached his new friends. Looking like a giant kitty cat with beautiful colors, as he came closer to Lezah and Maya he wished them hello and good morning.

Neither Maya nor Lezah had any fear of Zephaniah and they began to embrace his presence as the most lovable animal and, powerful protector in the rain forest.

5

WHEN KNOWLEDGE IS GIVEN

Hazel then spoke to Maya, Lezah, and Zephaniah. "I realize that nothing in life is handed to you. Go after those things you have a strong passion for. And as for knowledge, that's the most honorable thing one can go after." Lezah went back toward the cave, and around the same area, she found some peppermint leaves. She was so excited about taking a shower down at the waterfall to start her day, she fell and dropped her leaves.

The water was cold at first but quickly warmed up. As she looked around for something to dry off with, the birds of the air gathered around and wrapped some large leaves tightly around her. She noticed lots of greenery and blue skies all around in every corner of the rain forest.

"Now that everyone is present," Hazel said, as Lezah and Maya gathered around her. "Themba will continue to search for your missing families, but class will begin today for both of you. I am a good teacher, as you all know, and I'm passionate about education."

Now that it's the beginning of a new day, let's begin by eating something that is healthy. Nourishment is necessary for the body and mind; it gives energy. "Right now," said Hazel, "let's allow ourselves to inhale the fresh breeze in silence."

And in a quiet whisper, Maya said to Lezah. "This is the most beautiful place I've ever seen." The two of them were feeling safe and loved, and being cared for this caused their hearts to open up. Hazel proceeded to speak; all ears were listening.

"Every day begins with the sun having the ability to shine on everything she sets her eyes on. Everything that is grown in our rain forest has been nurtured by the sun.

We have abundant gifts of fruits like avocados, coconuts, figs, lemons, grapefruit, bananas, guavas, pineapples, mangos and tomatoes; some vegetables, including winter squash, and yams; and spices like cayenne, peppermint, cinnamon, cloves, ginger, and turmeric. These gifts keep us healthy and can be used as medicine in some cases of emergencies."

Hazel allowed the silence to pass through and then said, "Bow your heads, my children, and say a prayer of gratitude and thanksgiving for what you have received and begin nurturing your body by the way of the universe." "The first lesson is to know that all fruits and greens that are planted here have seeds that grow; therefore, nothing is ever wasted.

There are fresh waterfalls all around as well as streams and ponds full of water. This is a common ground for survival in all essences of life. After we have eaten, we will prepare ourselves to focus on who and what surrounds us, who lives in our environment. And how to get along with the many other different species that dwell in and around our tropical forest."

"Looking into our geography, we live in a river delta in Africa, not far above the beautiful mountains. The location is on the lower reaches of the rivers where the flow of water spreads out and slows down, depositing a peaceful flow into expanses of wetlands and shallow water. There are two types of deltas: coastal delta, where the river meets the sea and an inland delta, where the river fills extensive floodplains and marshes."

"Water lilies, grow nearly everywhere, and the type of water lily depends on which geographical regions in the world you are visiting. Water lilies can survive all climates, while tropical water lilies can only handle tropical climates. Water lilies grow in water, and the most obvious place is in a pond, but beneath the water surface, there are pods that hold the soil and the water lily seeds."

"Please tell me more," said Maya, as she became engrossed in the life of the water lily. "Well," Hazel paused, "I will continue, my child. The next lesson to be learned is to never interrupt without expressing a "Pardon me, please."

"Pardon me," said Maya to Miss Hazel.

Maya was flying so carelessly that she managed to bump into Hymesee, an egret. Hymesee looked like a tall duck on stilts, her long legs moving very fast as she tried to keep up while listening to Hazel. And who is this strange bird, with legs so strong and long? thought Lezah.

Hazel could read Maya's thoughts. She was thinking. She looks like a duck with stilts and a Pinocchio nose. "My child, you are so funny," Hazel said. "Why do you continue to look so surprised? Hymesee is among our friends here. And you Lezah what are you thinking right now?"

"Only that I am so open to learn more and meet more friends in your rain forest." With her bright smile, Lezah looked over at Maya. Then Lezah turned to look around and spotted a beautiful dragonfly.

"Who are you?" asked Lezah.

"My name is Sammobia. I'm a dragonfly. I've been flying above your head for a while now." Hazel then said, "I guess you heard someone call your name, Lezah." "Yes, I did, Miss Hazel," said Lezah. "She's a beautiful dragonfly."

"Everything here is so beautiful the creatures of the air, on land, and waters here and around the pond." Enough. My children, stop trying hard to mirror someone who is not yourself. Stay in your zone and learn to embrace and love who you are. "Be a good version of yourself."

"It's difficult," said Maya.

"I know," said Hazel. "You will get there." Sometimes you have to put in some work. I mean, put hard work into everything you do in life to give it your best. I promise you will get there.

"Have you all met Tryrome? He happens to be our very slow rattlesnake that loves moving about in the shallow waters. He enjoys placing all encounters on his surprise list as he slowly wraps his body around the stones and small bushes in the water. He loves playing the part of a smooth operator along with playing possum. Sometimes he likes to catch you off guard by rambling through the bushes and stopping when you pause to allow you to think you heard something. Then he appears to say 'boo' but instead he says in a whisper, 'hello,' and how are you?"

"And look, there's Codlebra, a medium dace fish. "Wow she looks invisible to me. Is that good?" said Lezah. "Ooh," said Maya I've never seen a fish quite like that ever before. "Amazing, it is," said, Hazel.

As things continued in the rain forest with Hazel, Maya, Lezah, Hymesee, Sammobia, Zephaniah, Tryrome and Codlebra, more things were in store.

Now back at Spider Webb Drive, things were not going as well. Lezah's mother Zora was now panicking; she hadn't heard from Lezah, and she should have been home from school. Lezah had been missing now for over twenty-four hours, and no one had a clue as to what was happening.

People were beginning to talk. Nothing like this had ever happened in the town of Rambling Woods. Because of this town being family friendly, nothing had ever gone unnoticed. Someone would be able to give you a story and facts about whatever may have happened in this small town.

The doorbell rang. With a tissue in her hand and fear in her voice, Zora allowed the police to come inside. As the officer asked questions, she found it hard to even think about how something like this could have happened to her daughter. It made her think of her mother's disappearance many years ago. And she didn't want to speculate that something like this would hit home once again.

How could this be happening? She thought as the tears ran down her cheeks. She couldn't envision any thoughts of her daughter being no longer in her life. The officer now asked for permission to check Lezah's room to see if they could find some clues.

Her bed was still made up. There was a book on her bed left open, and Zora noticed something strange about the book. So with no questions to ask the police, she closed the book and placed it back on Lezah's desk beside the other noticeable books of discovery she had in place.

They found no clues, and the officer told Zora that they would take this investigation seriously and work hard to find out what, why, and how Lezah disappeared. Zora went back in Lezah's room and sat on her bed, clutched her favorite stuffed animal, and inhaled the lavender scent in her daughter's room. She wanted her baby to come home or find a way to let her know that she was okay.

6

CAPTURING THE BEAUTY
OF WATERFALL BAY

It was so calming and relaxing out in the forest and the view was impeccable. "Look," Maya said to Lezah, "a waterfall." Lezah smiled and said, "Yes, it's awesome! I had a chance to bathe in that waterfall this morning."

Maya asked Miss Hazel, "Can we please go down to the waterfalls?" The whispering breeze touched them as they approached the falls. They could smell the combined scents of vegetation, moisture, and plants. And the red cedarwood trees gave off the scent of a cedar chest and crushed fruit that permeated the air.

After getting close to the waterfall, everyone was able to enjoy a breathtaking moment. The education process continued about education, for there was still a lot to be learned and accomplished before Maya could be a human. Before Lezah arrived in the rain forest, Hazel thought that Maya would be her only protégé but now it had doubled to two.

On the other hand, Hazel had some strong feelings in her spirit about Lezah. She was feeling some attachment to her even though Lezah kept more to herself and did not chatter as much as Maya the butterfly.

"And so," said Hazel, "nothing is ever handed to us on silver or gold spoon unless you were born with a gold or silver spoon in your mouth. That simply means that you are lucky enough to be born rich."

"You see, being rich doesn't necessarily mean that much when your health is failing or you lose your family. You generate lots of false friends only because of what you have or what you can give. Is it better to be rich in mind, body, and spirit? Tell me, what do you think?"

"Miss Hazel," said Lezah, "I think that having the right mind-set to be educated about inheritance allows you to earn the value of your riches. Therefore, everything about this kind of wealth will take you to a trusting and honest way to survive and attract true friends."

Then Maya finished by saying, "Those friends who are true to themselves first will come into your life without you ever having to look for them. They will find you as a friend."

"So true," said Hazel, "you both shared some very strong answers to support the question.

I feel that now you are listening and learning at the same time. Much like here in Waterfall Bay, it's all about health, wealth in the spirit of love, building support, being creative, and sharing. So many other things can contribute to make things better, but love is the greatest and most vital of all things to treasure."

Suddenly, Lezah finds herself going in and out of existence. She feels almost invisible at times. As the day was winding down, she felt a drop of rain. Then it began to drizzle a bit, so they took cover under some of the big leaves. Once again, Lezah felt strange, as if she was fading. It was like something unreal. It was as though she had no presence and could not be seen.

So, with a quiet voice, she asked Miss Hazel if she could go back to the cave and get some rest, for she was tired and worn out for some reason she couldn't understand. She didn't want anyone to know what she was feeling. She was now in the center of discovering her newfound powers, as her gifts.

It was difficult because she wanted to own what she had discovered, but the concept was not clear enough for her to understand. At this point her life was going through some kind of change.

And she didn't want anyone to know, especially, Miss Hazel, believing that she would become a distraction. Hazel was going in and out as well. She was taking on her human form and then turning back into the huge water lily.

Since nightfall was coming and everyone was getting tired, no one saw the changes that Hazel was experiencing. As for the others, they found their resting places, leaving Maya and Zephaniah going back to the cave. Maya found the perfect spot right next to Lezah and covered Lezah's body with her wings for warmth throughout the night till morning. Zephaniah again curled up closer to Lezah and Maya, and they all soon fell asleep.

That next day, Lezah realized that since she had arrived in the rain forest, she had never heard the sounds of laughter coming from children playing. In a polite voice, she whispered to Miss Hazel, "Where are the children?"

Making close eye contact, Hazel's responded, "The children are in safe havens for now. Some years ago, there was war on this planet. It was very bad; so bad that it was difficult to speak about and to tell what really happened. The children brought laughter, simplicity, and love, but it wasn't enough for that planet to hold strong."

"The ruler Jubu was a hated man who thrived on breaking down the bridges, towers, roads, and rock-solid cement that the municipality was built on. For several years, fear was brought into the lives of so many that were hoping to see a new day. That new day never came. In fact, the ruler before Jubu was Piroc, who stirred up so much turmoil that the other megacity Zengorra began to build up hatred as well."

"Everything about the megacity, before the new rule came, was peaceful with high energy and love for one another, and kindness was shown to it's people worldwide. With shades of so many colors, the rich, middle class, and poor were kind and respectful. No shame was thrown on any class of people because of the umbrella of love. There was work for all who needed labor. This allowed everyone to feel well-adjusted.

"Of course, the only difference was that the rich lived high on hills, the middle class lived in their own peaceful valley, and the poor lived among their own terrain. However, there were rules and laws that were made up by the people, for the people, and everyone respected them."

"Love of life and the life of others led to their strong beliefs as they learned to live in their peaceful environments.

Then came the weapons, which were of hate, and the aftermath destroyed all living things, leaving nothing standing and no survivors only those children that were found broken, scarred, and gifted."

Hazel realized that Lezah was trying hard to figure out how to ask her "what was meant by a child being gifted." She continued to inform her of more details about the destruction in order to keep her from asking any questions that would need more explaining. Right now was not yet the time.

As Hazel continued to speak, she addressed an issue that she did not want to share at this time. "It took many years for this land to rebuild itself. Everything was destroyed. Jubu played a big part in the destruction."

"Who is this Jubu?" asked Lezah. Miss Hazel said, "He's the ruler of the planet Xenotopia, who continues to cause destruction by stealing the Orbs of Life. "As a leader, he has failed his people. And their land has not been prospering for some time now.

Jubu is a human shape-shifter, known to be very clever. He tends to keep his ability to himself.

He believes that he is one of a kind with the ability to physically transform into monsters, and with super human ability, divine intervention, and demonic manipulation. He can heal nonfatal wounds, and even replace body parts such as his ears or a big piece of skin.

Along with intervention or magic, he controls humans, animals, and all insects in the air and on land. Hazel fears that Jubu was given information about Lezah and her presence in the rain forest, because Jubu wants to control both worlds, Xenotopia and Earth.

"I have said too much already," said Hazel. "We must not move away from what we are trying to learn, for right now is not the time." Lezah, in a frightened voice, whispered, "When will be the right time, Miss Hazel?"

Back in Rambling Woods, Lezah's mother was comforting herself by being around people she knew and loved in her workplace at the hospital.

She had found it painful to eat or sleep, so she chose to keep busy helping those who could not help themselves. As a nurse, it allowed her to stay at the hospital and take on more shifts instead of going home.

The hospital had made provisions for her to sleep over whenever it was needed. Her neighbors were good watchdogs working together for any sighting of Lezah in or around the area. Actually, some neighbors would take turns staying in her home, in case Lezah returned.

As Zora finished her shift, it allowed her to put things in perspective and try to figure out what could have happened on that day her daughter disappeared.

She had made contact with Lezah on the same day of her disappearance to let her know that she would be arriving home a few hours late. And everything seemed to be okay. Lezah never mentioned to her mom that something was wrong. All was good on the home front.

Zora closed her eyes to try to understand why she didn't take the time to check her daughter's room as she always did in saying good night.

She would tuck her in every night with a kiss embossed on her forehead. But what happened on that night for something like this to happen? Was it because she was too tired to look in on Lezah?

Question after question came up, and there seemed to be no answers. What was the reasoning of her disappearance? Was it something she did or did not do that may have caused this to happen?

She just couldn't make any light of day, so this had become the darkest time in her life. When she did go home, she would burn her candle and pray for hours, hoping that something would turn up.

7

LESSONS ARE LEARNED

The police were on the case as well, and still nothing turned up. Not even one clue could be found. So much is happening again, she thought. She couldn't allow herself to break down and become sick by not eating and blame herself and not get enough rest.

At some points, she felt that Lezah would never return, disappearing just like her mother had many years ago. So she opened Lezah's bedroom door and started to search for clues. She kept in mind that she was not going to stop searching until she found something. She looked through her closet, under the bed, on her desk and chest, and then her jewelry box; Lezah's necklace was not in the box.

Right before her daughter's tenth birthday, her mom presented her with a gift box. Inside was a sterling silver heart divided into two: one section of the heart read "Zora my mother," and the other part of the heart read "Lezah my daughter."

Her mother was wearing her necklace with the inscription "Lezah my daughter." Therefore, she knew Lezah was wearing her necklace. So now, Zora felt that she had something that would come in handy for the police.

She continued to look for more information that would be helpful to give to the police. There was a book on Lezah's desk that was hard to overlook. It's appearance was very strange. It was an old, rustic-looking book not like the other book on her desk. It had a strange cover. There was a giant water lily in a pond surrounded by fish, a large plain butterfly, an eagle, a dragonfly, a rattlesnake, a panther, and some kind of a tall bird.

Oh, wait, she thought, there's a little girl in this picture. Staring long and hard at the picture of the little girl, she shook her head saying, "No, that can't be." She appeared to resemble Lezah. "She has my daughter's hair, and that outfit the girl is wearing is exactly like Lezah's. It's one of a kind. My mother hand made that outfit, and she made it too big. Therefore, it took some years before Lezah could wear it."

She then checked her daughter's closet just to make sure and found that too was gone. There was no other pattern out there like that outfit. "Oh my God, she is wearing Lezah's necklace."

"No, that can't be my daughter in that picture. No, that can't be my baby girl, Lezah, in that picture on the cover of a strange book.

Lezah my baby girl, what is happening?"

As she opened the book, the doorbell rang, and there was a knock at the same time. She closed the book and ran downstairs, hoping that it would be some good news about her daughter.

As she opened the door, Zora saw a gathering of neighbors all wanting to help find Lezah. Some brought hand-prepared meals, as they knew she put in long hours at work and looked rather frail and a bit thin since this all happened. Zora was so overwhelmed with excitement just to think that some of these people she barely knew had formed a crew to help out.

She allowed them to come inside, and with her eyes filled with tears, she said, "I just don't know where to begin. My daughter has been missing for days now, and I just want her back home."

With all the commotion going on, Zora totally forgot about the book she was about to open and went upstairs to get the most recent photo of her daughter, Lezah.

Coming downstairs, she smiled and said, "Maybe we can start by circulating her photo around the neighborhood. And then we can check with some of her friends."

She had never met any of Lezah's friends. Her daughter had never brought anyone home for her mom to meet, so her next step was to check out some of her classmates from school. Zora's days seemed to be so long, yet each day that went by was painful to get through. This is so strange. How could something like this happen?

That next morning she took a personal day from work to speak with the principal at her daughter's school. She thought it was strange, because Lezah was not marked absent, and none of her teachers had any idea that she was missing.

"I am the principal here at this school, and I didn't have any idea that this had happened. You must be thinking where my accountability is, in this situation, if she had been taken during school hours. Each of her teachers spoke very highly of Lezah. "Even though she's a new student, she had been doing very well so far," stated, Principal McKinney.

However, Lezah was never sought after by friends because she kept to herself as she attended her classes here at her new school. "Mrs. Hany," said Principal McKinney, "I'm hearing from her teachers that she is up to date with classwork." "I am so sorry that this happened. Is there anything I can do to help?" "Principal McKinney," said Zora, "The police are working hard on her case, and thank you for your time."

Little did anyone notice, that Lezah was gifted. She made herself present in her homeroom and her classes. And she would disappear whenever she found the need to find things outside of school that caught her interest like the library and discover things outside the neighborhood that would allow her to reach home on time, as school let out.

Zora left the school and journeyed home to find her front door ajar. She wasn't afraid to enter because she knew her neighbors would be close by. So she entered, closing the door behind her. She wandered into the living room, kitchen, and dining area to find that no one was there. So she went upstairs and saw no one in any of the rooms. Maybe she left the door ajar as she was hurrying to get to the school.

What is going on? she thought, as she began to remember her mother and the stories that people told about her back when she was a young child. It was said that Zora's mother had a dark side, and that there were dark secrets and lies told out of kindness rather than to deceive or be malicious about her mother. Maybe it was deeper than that. Could my mother be involved in this?

Now, Hazel moved forward and shared with her students. "You all may not know that the owls and nighthawks awaken when the sun sets and hunt and help out at night.

"The other animals of the land began to inhale fresh, pure oxygen from the new rebirth of the air in a clean fresh environment. There were those that began creating a new city. They were not afraid of hard work. They worked hard during the night into the darkness, straight into the morning."

"During the daytime, they found a safe place and closed their eyes to block out the light. In contrast, there were other animals that are diurnal, meaning they are awake during the day and sleep at night. Everyone has a part in building this new and improved city. It's being built as I'm speaking now.

The dark allowed them to work into the light to reveal the images of a city, which was in the process of being built with much-needed love, strength, support, confidence, and happiness for all people.

"The new world structure would be nothing like any other; it was being built on a new foundation. There was a vision of a strong capital city that would produce new and exciting things into a new generation."

Maya spoke out, "Where are... I mean, where then are the human people that will be living among the animals, the gifted, and the insect creatures of every kind?" "Is there an architectural design or drawing to help create this new rebirth of a strong capital city to come?"

"It's all been designed in the formation of things to come my child." "Be still, Maya, and listen," said Hazel.

"I have some very strong spiritual insight of the highest form of wisdom that I will give to you only once." "As you seek to take on a human form, remember that the biggest burden to carry around is fear. Let it go and allow the highest source to work with you. A fool is one who throws away the mind-set with the ability to learn or to be educated.

Doing what you think is right is always the smarter and wiser way to go. Stay away from liars. They are very dangerous. The ones who will make you want to learn are the good teachers you will find along your way as you travel through life. Never surround yourself among complainers. You will always be disagreeable in everything and with everyone."

8

A LIGHT ON WISDOM

"**A**lways believe in yourself and know that your best day is today, and your best work will be what you master in life," Hazel said. "And your comfort will become the knowledge that you have done your work well."

"And don't allow your soul to become bankrupt, for you will have lost all enthusiasm. And feeling bad about others' success will only give you the meanest treasures you could ever reach for as you try to succeed. Don't allow your mistake to give you a means to give up fighting for what you believe in.

Never indulge in hate but have the Most High as your greatest thought. Finding fault with others is the stupidest thing to do. Don't allow yourself to stoop that low, for you will become a troublemaker. You need common sense in all things. Don't allow your life to become a puzzle that can carry you through the greatest mystery, which is a dead end."

"And lastly know that what lies deep within your heart, mind, and spirit is the greatest thing in the world: "love.""

"Now with all of that being said, "Maya, always stay true to yourself," and honor yourself by knowing that who you are is a special gifted one."

"And now I want to say we have another highly gifted child to speak about, who never knew she had those special gifts. Come closer, Lezah, whose name is Hazel when spelled backward."

"That's my grandmother's name," said Lezah. "My mother said I was named after her mother, but she never told me her name was Hazel. I thought my grandmother's name was Lezah too."

"No, my child, it is I."

"I am your grandmother. My name is Hazel."

"Suddenly, Lezah found it unbelievable at first as she looked at Hazel as a water lily.

"Are you really my grandmother?"

"Yes, I am. And I have a lot of explaining to do, my child. You see, Lezah, I am a human."

Before she could continue to explain to Lezah, she was interrupted by Themba, the African bald eagle, who surprised her with her return to give Hazel the news of what she had discovered in her mission to find Maya's family. "Themba, what did you find?" "Hazel, my finding is limited because of the continuing wars."

The planet Butari has a city named Avaszion, where war has destroyed so much and is still ongoing. I managed to lose my way and stumble onto this beautiful planet's city. I have seen birds and insects of the air that were among many other foreign species, who have elected to help in such magnitude that has become critical as a mega-war taking place. However, help is desperately needed at this time in those war zone areas.

"Creatures of the air, flying insects and their allies were working together to save the city of Avaszion. Much of the devastation has taken over the metropolis of Zengorra, with the desire to take control of the entire planet of Butari."

"Everything is in an uproar. Loyalty is no more. The smell of chemical and toxic waste is in the air."

"It has become a place emptied of all things, a deserted areas. Seeing flocks of birds with broken and shattered wings and ripped out hearts, their spirits are tattered and helpless throughout all this uprising. The city of Zengorra has taken control and power from all the flying creatures and insects."

Before sharing anything further, Themba asked that Maya and Lezah go down to the waterfall with Hymesee and wait for Hazel there. She assured them that Hazel would accompany them down at the waterfall later. Hazel also kept in mind that no news is good news, as she saw Themba's face as a sign that something was wrong. It was important that nothing else be mentioned until they both headed down to the waterfalls with Hymesee.

Themba continued in a whisper to Hazel about how she had seen over sixty extant species of flightless birds, including the well-known rarities: ostriches, emus, cassowaries, rheas, kiwis, and penguins. All were wounded. Even the smallest flightless birds were scattered, frail, wounded, lost, and to be forgotten.

Themba didn't want to upset Maya, so Hymesee distracted her while Themba spoke to Hazel.

They did not want Maya to know that her father was found wounded in the city of Avaszion. Her brother, Adonis, was found safe, and her mother was in Avaszion attending to her husband's wounds. Both her parents are high-ranking officials on the planet of Butari as well.

"The beauty of the planet was being destroyed," Themba said. "I've never seen a more beautiful place made with rocks, of gold roads lined with sterling silver, and stones made of pearls, emeralds, mineral, and aluminum in some areas. All being destroyed, there lived a kaleidoscope of butterflies, armies of caterpillars, charms of hummingbirds, and winged beetles, namely fireflies or lighting bugs known for their rainbows of colors. There are about five thousand species of lady bugs and, beautiful praying mantises, and flocks of many kinds of birds of the air.

"Maya and her brother come from a family of Queen Alexandra bird wing butterflies. They are said to be the largest butterflies in the world. They're majestic and quite beautiful. They can blend into their environment and are able to protect themselves by making it hard to be seen or spotted.

They have a way to camouflage themselves by siting on branches of trees without any notion of being recognized. The male's wings are smaller than the females, yet the male has a more colorful, bright yellow stomach with green and aquamarine wings, while the female is dark brown with blue and green markings with a yellow stomach."

Hazel then said, "Thank you for a job well done as always, Themba."

While Hazel was trying to place her thoughts in the right direction, her eyes moved toward the waterfall to locate Maya and Lezah as they were playing. She thought this butterfly is free from the elements of hardship, pain, and responsibilities but lost in the spirit of finding true happiness. Her adamant desire as a butterfly is to be a child.

She would give her all just to be human, childlike, innocent, and full of grace, allowing her to send out nothing other than pure love to the whole world. My heart goes out to Maya, who will soon know that her home and family are in a state of war.

Hazel turned and looked at Themba.

"What do we do now?

How do we tell Maya, Themba?" "What caused such a war to fumigate the air with so much rant and rave?"

"What I can put together, Hazel, is that this has been about the orbs, a spiritual body, a glow that lives among the cities, planets, and all dwellings. It gives life and feeds into life and prosperity on each planet. Without this existence, a city or planet loses its oxygen.

These wars are stirring up all over, and they are all about having domain among the powerful species and turf having the wealth of the planet of Butari and the planet city of Avaszion."

This changes a lot of things, Hazel thought. And to put things right, she would have to reveal a longtime secret that had been hidden from her confidants, closest friends, and all other creatures in the Amazonika rain forest, in which she made home to so many and named Waterfall Bay.

Hazel (a.k.a. Unee) was a human. She was gifted with many strong abilities, telepathy, teleportation, and shape-shifting and her human name was Unee. She was known as the guardian to many while others had no idea of her transformation.

As a giant water lily, she had adapted a way of protecting herself by growing thorns on the bottom of her leaves to protect her from fishes and, other predators that might want to eat at her. These rims protected her leaves from birds and insects that might want to eat the leaves in or around her pad, and it became a barrier.

When Hazel first arrived and teleported herself into the rain forest, she found Elias a boy left behind with the gift of telepathy by his parents. He had shown evidence of high-performance capabilities.

He was intellectual and, creative, with leadership capacities in every specific academic field. He was well-versed in services that would be needed for him to reign. And he had always gained knowledge from Unee as his guardian, in order to fully develop his capabilities and skills.

Unee was considered the guardian of all those children, especially the ones gifted with telepathy and teleportation, among many other abilities.

9

STORY OF NO RETURN

Not understanding, Hazel thought, Why hadn't I noticed Lezah's capabilities when she first arrived in Waterfall Bay? There were no signs, no signals, indicating her gifts like the others. How well she hid those things that I missed upon her arrival. Lezah found a way to camouflage herself so that no one could see the obvious, which were her gifts.

How brilliant that she could not imagine anything like this happening, and she wanted to share with the others. Hazel would have liked to have calculated her thoughts on the different gifts that were seen by both Lezah and Maya in their experiences.

Hazel seemed to lose sight as to who she really was at this point as well. "Both are gifted as I see it," said Hazel to Themba. "We must keep them safe." Only a few knew of Unee's transformation as a human, and her disguise as Hazel, the water lily. Hazel spoke in a language created from pig Latin, and her memories as a child were a made-up language.

It was formed from English by transferring the initial consonant or consonants cluster of each word to the end of the word and adding a vocalic syllable. So, chicken soup would be translated to "ickenchay oupsay" which would be clearly identified and was taught to all the gifted children who caught on so fast and mastered this skill of communicating with each other.

"Now is the time, Themba, for you to travel to the new metropolis of Neferzion. This name included the last four letters of Zion, who was favored to rule Quantazaire when it is built. This city will be populated with humans, the gifted, many animals great and small, and a variety of birds of the air, land, and sea. It will be unlike any other city ever built. Our gifted ones will play a big part in the configuration of the completion of all things."

"Themba, I need you to find the principle builder and ask him to meet with me here along with the others. I need to see newly added rough or unfinished drawings to allow us to see more of the finished picture of the new city." "Right away," said Themba. "I will go at once and bring back what is asked of me."

As Hazel walked toward the waterfall, Maya and Lezah were laughing and playing together. When they saw Hazel coming, they started running to meet her. Hymesee seemed to be buried deep in her thoughts after giving into what she had seen and felt near the waterfall. Hazel headed toward Hymesee at the waterfall, and looking straight into her eyes, she could see something was wrong.

"Hymesee, are you okay?" asked Hazel.

"Yes, I think so," said Hymesee. "I thought I saw Lezah do something unusual. And I want to share that with you. What I have to say may sound crazy, and you might think it is nonsense." As Lezah and Maya continued their laughing, Sammobia, the dragonfly, got their attention to delay them while Hazel seemed to be in a serious conversation with Hymesee. This allowed Hymesee to confront Hazel with what she thought she saw Maya and Lezah doing that was a bit strange.

"You know, Hazel," said Hymesee, "both Maya and I were talking about her brother. It was like she teleported him, and I became him, and I wasn't me."

We were sharing things as well as being transported into a place I've never seen. There was much laughter and beautiful things that I never thought existed in our time. Then I managed to see Lezah talking to her grandmother; they were so happy.

Lezah is a curious little girl. She said to me, "I know the voice of my grandmother, and I know she is here with me. I could see her." It was you, Hazel. It was a picture of you— a silhouette seen within the waterfalls-- and it was very real.

"Being in the midst of these two was enlightening, endearing, and different. In fact, it was a wonderful experience, yet it was strange. How can something be viewed as a lifetime when it was only a few seconds of my time summoned in a dream? I'm still puzzled as to what really happened. I guess, Hazel I'll never know."

With a smile and nothing else to say, Hazel proceeded to share with Hymesee that everyone would soon be meeting at the pond.

This meant that Hazel would have to expose Elias and the others who had been hidden in Neferzion, even though Quantazaire was being built and there has always been some kind of common housing for the gifted. No one had ever seen the gifted in Waterfall Bay.

That was because they were all housed in Neferzion. Much would be exposed at the gathering around the pond. And, of course, Hazel would have to tell her story from the very beginning, explaining why she kept such a big secret among those she pulled together as family and her closest friends.

Even Mr. Sun, who continued to shine brightly everyday upon Waterfall Bay, was surprised. And to think that all this was taking place under the bright light from his source of positive sunshine.

Mr. Sun was totally prepared for this meeting to gain knowledge about what was going on around the Amazonika rain forest in Waterfall Bay, along with information about the news of a city called Quantazaire being built in the capital city of Neferzion.

As everyone gathered around the pond, the meeting began. All creatures great and small, on land and sea, had to get reacquainted with one another. This was the first meeting in the rain forest to be called to order at Waterfall Bay. There was complete silence. Nothing could be heard, and everyone was waiting for Hazel to come and show herself on her huge lily pad.

Suddenly, her voice was heard loud and very strong. It was a voice, that was never heard by all in the Amazonika rain forest of Waterfall Bay. This was her human voice, as "Unee." Then she transformed into a human right before the eyes of everyone present.

Some thought it was amazing, and some thought it was a kind of magic trick she had conjured up for this meeting, while others thought to take it all in and simply try to understand as much as possible. This was really an eye opener for Hymesee, all because she thought she saw Maya do the same thing. Then she thought, am I losing my mind?

What just happened?

Hazel was opening up and exposing what needed to be revealed.

"This was a long time coming," she said.

There was a stillness as she spoke. It was unbelievable, what was being said. It was inconceivable that no one knew or was aware of this. They all thought they knew her so well and that she shared so much. Little did they know Hazel gave them only what she thought they needed to know. In the blink of an eye, Hazel transformed into a woman of flawless beauty, a radiant human in a gown molded in colors never seen before. Her glow allowed everyone to become speechless and amazed.

It was mystical to see the most inspiring transformation take place in Waterfall Bay. They were thinking. Why did she keep this hidden from all of us? Did she not trust and love us enough to let us in on this dual lifestyle? Everyone was still silent, not knowing that her mission was to build a new nation that would be highly global because of the destruction of everything around.

Maybe this allowed her to do her best work in keeping things hidden. They had no idea that something could be developing in this new world that would be greater and more advanced than any other world, nation, or planet.

Hazel continued to speak about what had been accomplished. She then spoke on a personal matter. "We live in a world of humans. There are many species who reside among us.

My life has always been, since birth, a human. My transformation has been the water lily. You see, my human side had to come out every day, so the best time was at night. "Elias was about five years old when I found him alone here in the rain forest, crying because he was lost.

We tried to find his parents, but not even a footprint could be found. And so I am his guardian. As a human I was able to raise Zion along with Elias as brothers. They would always play together and learn how to use their gifts. They were a great comfort to me, as I missed my daughter and granddaughter deeply after I disappeared."

"Elias grew to be an excellent assistant in all things related to human forms and functions, telepathy, and the theoretical transfer of matter or energy from one point to another without traversing the physical space between them."

10

SENSIBILITY

"However," Hazel continued, "Zion, my biological son, grew as well to become totally in charge and to master his skills to develop his telepathy in making good of his gifts."

"Zion would transform while I didn't even know he was blessed with such amazing qualities. He was inquisitive and curious. He taught Elias and me the simple things that became a big part in wanting to make the rain forest our home. I would see things that were made useful, and we were able to learn quite a bit. Zion is brilliant and, self-taught, and he continues to educate the gifted little ones who are learning so rapidly how to use their powers as gifts. Zion and Elias made my life as a water lily much easier here at Waterfall Bay. Long after, I was able to place them in the safe house to continue my life here as a water lily without anyone knowing till now."

"Allow me to say this: life will never fail you, if you take time to correct your mistakes along the way.

Because those mistakes in your life will catch up to you, so be sure that you know your way, be prepared to do the right things, and know who you are and the direction in which you're going."

Silence was felt all around. Eyes and ears were focused on Hazel as she continued to speak about her role as a human with the help and support she got from Zion and Elias. Both young men gave her so much encouragement. As she spoke, she would glance at them with a smile. Because for a long time they had been the only family she knew, as she began to build a stronger family in the rain forest. Then her eyes focused on Lezah with a smile and, she announced that Lezah is her granddaughter.

Hazel then said, "Maya I want to express regret for something I did to you when you landed in my pond. I was so exhausted from transforming back from a human to the water lily that I became disturbed, even though you were humble in asking me for help. I really didn't mean to hurt this lost butterfly who came to me with such a big heart. Maya didn't deserve my actions and response.

"All Maya wanted was to rest while asking for help to find her family and to become a human at the same time. However, it developed into an episode that almost turned her into a human child, but something in my spirit was so exhausted that I blamed the unlucky experience on Maya. She really thought it was her fault."

"At this time, please allow me to say. "Maya, I'm sorry that I allowed you to think all of this was your fault. Can you find it in your heart to forgive me?" "Yes, I forgive you, Miss Hazel," Maya said. The group applauded.

"Maya, come forward. We have found your parents. Your father has been wounded, and your mother and brother both are okay and are waiting for you as soon as the war ends. There is still a high volume of losses but in the meantime, we are building up a new city called Quantazaire not far from your homeland of Avaszion.

Themba gave us this news yesterday and we were cautious about many things. We wanted to wait until you were ready to receive this information. Now that everything is out in the open, we will make a way for you to stay and be among family and friends here.

"You are gifted, Maya, and it's time for you to make use of those gifts. You will learn to use them well. There is no rose garden in life, but there are many gardens out there that have had prosperous growth."

How is it, Maya, that your parents never knew of your gifts? You are so gifted that you were able to become that little girl anytime your heart desired.

"In fact, you were the key to your parents, along with your brother, in making positive transformations that would allow them to discover their own rights in becoming and maintaining a life of who they are now or taking on a human form. And, yes, your family was also able to take on human forms.

I'm sure your parents are aware that the universe gives us a time frame to elevate our skills and make good use of our most precious gift: time."

It was all becoming clear to Maya now.

Maya believed that her parents were aware of her gifts; however, they didn't want anything to influence her innocence as a child in taking on a human form.

Hazel was a bit reluctant to continue to speak on Maya's behalf, because everyone present had been waiting for the truth of Hazel's dual presence as a water lily and a human. "How was this possible?" asked, Themba. "I oversaw everything during the day and night, and I have mastered my skills to be the best as your security."

So, for now, Hazel had to take everyone present back to when she first arrived in the rain forest. She made it clear that she had transported herself there not knowing anything about this place.

She was with child and very much human, and after giving birth to her son, Zion, she developed her ability to adopt new forms and personas to maintain her existence in a positive way. She loved water lilies and always believed that if she had a second life, she would come back as a beautiful water lily. And why not be one if it was at all possible?

"So that is what I did," Hazel said. "Perhaps it's not clear to you; however, please continue to listen and allow me to explain why I chose to transform myself into a water lily and kept my human side hidden."

"I will begin by addressing the fact that turning into a water lily allowed me to be safe. People would find their way into the rain forest to see the beautiful waterfalls, and I was afraid of being seen or questioned about living here. So, at night, Elias and Zion would help me to redirect and reinforce new trails in other directions, so that there could be no signs that would lead people into the rain forest.

Now that this place did not exist for anyone outside to come in as a tourist, I was able to give this area the name "Waterfall Bay." We've done such good work in secluding the forest, and it has become my home for many seasons. Truth be told, this has been how I've survived as a waterlily. I hope you all can pardon me for all the deceptions."

Lezah looked on with many questions, but looking at her grandmother, things were becoming clearer. Her eyes focused on a view, and like magic it was as if she could see a window of memories taking her back home, where she was seated beside her grandmother.

"Miss Hazel," "you are my grandmother. Tell me why you left my mother and me to disappear to never be in our lives. Please tell me, Grandmother. Why?"

Hazel said, "My child, I've always loved you and your mother, and you were missed so much. I will tell you this. One night, an entity entered my room while I was asleep, and something happened. I became with child.

And for that reason, I moved on. I knew no one would understand why or how that happened, I could not make any sense of it myself. I also knew that I had many gifts, and one was to teleport myself here into the rain forest. I was human, and I had to struggle to survive and raise my son, Zion, all alone.

You have an uncle, and your mother has a brother. After many years had passed, I found out that Jubu is Zion's father. And so for years I managed to stay hidden in the rain forest. Zion is safe now as I was able to find a safe haven for many of our gifted ones, some animal and others human."

"Grandmother, where is Zion's father?" asked Lezah.

"I wish I knew," said Hazel. "And you my child," have all the power in the world to go back home without my help."

Lezah, we must start from scratch to light your way, and you were named after me. "Have you learned to use any of your gifts?"

"No, Grandmother," Lezah said. "I was never told that I had any such gifts or powers." Her grandmother responded with a smile. "We have no power, my child. We have gifts. And how is it that you never detected anything surprising, different, or uncommon about yourself, Lezah? Did you not wonder how easy it was for you to take a deep breath and get to another place? Or did you think your library book had magical powers?"

"Grandmother, I really thought the book had magic, and it was the main source of me being here."

"Lezah," said her grandmother, "I placed the book in the library there so that you would come to me."

"You did, Grandmother. Is that why I also disappeared? So that Mommy couldn't find me?" "No, no, Granddaughter, not at all." And with eyes filled with tears, her grandmother said, "It was meant for both of you to come."

11

THE CLASH OF THE ORBS

Then Lezah shared that she didn't want her mother to know she had the book because of the adventure she first found while reading.

"Lezah, at your school, did you ever find it strange that you never met any friends and you were always alone?"

"You would attend classes, and with your mind telepathy you passed every test with high scores and were known as the most outstanding student in the whole school, even though you were noticed by the other students. They were curious about your presence there in the school."

"My child, your classmates could sense that you were special, and for that reason you were unapproachable.

Right now you are still a bit young to understand most of things I'm sharing with you."

"Your energy right now is so high because you want to know more, and you want to use your gifts to the fullest."

"Lezah my child, right now you feel as if you are riding on a bike with training wheels. There is no need to go any faster, for you will learn every function of the bike before the training wheels are removed.

In time, my child, in time there will be many things that will happen, and then you will be able to understand, I promise. I promise."

Just then a cloud of dust entered the sky as you could hear the sound of loud voices and a military raid of insects. It was a brigade of outsiders flying across the sky, causing havoc.

"Quickly now," said Hazel, "go and get into the caves. Take shelter quickly now, while I summon Elias to see what is taking place."

Elias is already heading toward the city of Butari, with smoke fill traces of elements lingering from the tail pipes of military vehicles as they traveled, which permeated throughout the air into the rain forest.

Themba had also summoned her army of well-trained eagles; other fighters in that territory were in human form carrying ammunition and guns. Loud explosions could be heard everywhere as Jubu's army stood their ground and waited for the word to strike.

Jubu and his army were searching for the Orbs of Life: stones of the highest elements for life's energy. Their search had been in the city of Butari, spilling into many of the surrounding smaller cities. Jubu had taken control of the outcasts,— those who were rejected, — and trained them to be soldiers who rained down mass destruction.

And to make matters worse, Jubu had been holding Elias's parents hostage. For years, Hazel believed that Elias was lost, but she later learned that Jubu had them abducted because of their close involvement with the orbs and their agricultural functions.

Bensarru and Lenefe knew they were being followed, and because of this, they hid Elias in the rain forest, hoping that someone good would find him.

Elias was left alone for several days in the rain forest, as his parents thought that they would be held for ransom then released to find their son.

Elias grew up thinking that they abandoned him, because they didn't want him.

When Themba heard about this, she was alarmed. Her guidelines have always been about safety in the highest rank of maximum security. She maintains everything on a high level and being totally responsible for the security of everything in and around the rain forest--up until Hazel had concealed all entrances.

There was no way in or out and this was to keep Waterfall Bay a safe haven for all those living within the range.

"How can this be," Elias asked Hazel, "when I was told that my parents had been killed?" A dream came to me that my father was trying to warn me of Jubu and his army. That dream was as true as I am standing here. It brought out the truth about why my parents had me hidden." "They were seized and then abducted by Jubu's men."

"They are alive residing in the city of Xenotopia under Jubu's jurisdiction and control." said Elias.

"At the same time," Jubu and his men were waiting on his ship, getting ready to take over the city of Butari.

"I am coming to seize the orb," Jubu shouted. "If it is not given willingly, we will take it."

Now, before Jubu could disembarked from the ship, the head consulate General Cinque confronted him and said, "Walk with me, so we can discuss this situation at hand.

What are your reasons for needing the architectural orb?"

Jubu said, "I need the orb to rebuild my city. It's becoming a wasteland. And my people have become oppressed and forgotten. This city of Butari has flourished enough! We want to take back what's ours!"

"I'm sorry to hear that, Jubu. Xenotopia had a small orb in the government towers," General Cinque replied.

"I'm aware of that, Cinque. That small piece of orb has burned out since this city started to rise, and once the orbs were burnt out, our buildings crumbled!"

"How is that possible? That small orb had enough energy to last for years to come," said General Cinque.

"That orb burned out because everyone left Xenotopia to come to Butari, and that's why we couldn't flourish. It seems that the orb burns out when people leave a city because the Orb's energy feeds on life," Jubu stated.

Themba continued to get her army into formation as they focused on going into battle to stop Jubu's army from seizing the orb.

They first needed to render help to the city of Butari, which was home to the tallest building. Its towers represented the government, the law, and the plight and structure of all existence of every planet.

As they headed toward the city, they found that Jubu was not far away. Some of Jubu's army were able to shapeshift and confiscate items that, if in the wrong hands, could cause a large amount of devastation.

Loud warning sirens were heard throughout the town.

All around were smoke-filled areas full of speeding vehicles with weapons and images of destruction.

Jubu stated, "Enough talk, Cinque.

I will give you two days to prepare your army for battle. The war will commence." "I'll take back what's mine."

He went back to his ship where his men were waiting, and they warped back into the city of Xenotopia. As time now does not wait, "no man is an island." For all is being destroyed by fear, and the traffic of many renegades is surfacing to take control.

Over a hundred military eagles that were sent to fight are in flight to journey into the battlefields of Jubu's army, not knowing that General Cinque and Jubu had agreed to take two days to get their armies ready for battle.

Hazel had a position overseeing the army she had built while residing in Waterfall Bay. They were being trained in the new city Quantazaire, in a location known for military use only.

This had become a high priority, as she had to prepare safety precautions for all those living in the rain forest.

She believed that the rain forest had no chance of being discovered; however, Hazel was not aware that Waterfall Bay was filled with rich resources in minerals, stones, gems and orbs.

12

TRUTH BE TOLD

Zora decided to go to Lezah's room to rediscover the book she had seen on her bed and later placed on her desk hoping to find a clue. As she approached the book, its cover seemed to be a bit different than when she first saw her daughter on the cover.

For some reason, the characters were no longer noticeable. It was as if they were fading from the cover. She wondered to herself, "Am I going crazy? My daughter was right on the cover of this book as clear as day." "What is going on?"

Zora proceeded to open the book to discover that it was telling a story that involved Lezah. She read on to find that a water lily was talking to a child about her daughter's age. Truth be told, she could only see the back of the child in the book.

Zora did not understand that she had the gift to teleport by closing her eyes and accepting the idea of traveling to another place.

She had been focusing on trying to find her daughter, which had made it impossible for her to get into the right mind-set. She continued to read on, fell asleep, and at the same time was transported into the rain forest, which she thought was a dream.

Everything now was so vivid and clear, but she did not see anyone else around. There was silence now in the rain forest. Only the flowing sounds of the waterfalls could be heard. She was not aware that there were wars going on and that everyone had been summoned by Hazel to go to their homes and find safety.

Zora woke up and did not realize she was actually in Waterfall Bay. She couldn't grasp mentally or understand again what just happened. What seemed like a dream was really reality.

It had been about three weeks now since her daughter's disappearance, and there were still no leads. So, she closed the book and went downstairs to prepare something to eat.

She turned on the news channel to check to see if there had been any other disappearances.

As she adjusted the TV, she heard them say that Lezah Hany was still missing, and they had no clues at this time. All that she could do was cry. Not knowing anything had her so severely overwhelmed with sadness. These last few weeks had left her unable to eat, sleep, or even work at her best.

As a sign of admiration, she would caress her half heart that she wore on a chain around her neck. This would seemingly give her some comfort as she would whisper,

"Lezah where are you? I need you to know that I love you and I miss you so much."

Zora then walked over to the pantry. On the shelf was a tin of her chamomile tea and a can of chicken noodle soup. As she prepared the soup for her dinner, she reached for a teacup to place her tea bag in as the teakettle was ready.

All of a sudden, she burnt her finger on the kettle, because she had a *déjà vu* that took her mind away from what she was doing. That book, that book is trying to tell me something.

She turned off the pot of soup while holding her cup of tea and ventured back upstairs to go through that book once again. She felt something uncanny just being in contact with this strange book. First, she noticed a little girl that looked like Lezah on the cover, and then she discovered that there were only images of what she thought she saw.

"How could that be?" she thought. Maybe my brain has a way of shifting things. Sometimes things are not what you think you see but what your mind creates. I thought I was asleep but that was not true, so I must have been in that rain forest after all.

She placed her cup on Lezah's night table and went into her room. She came back with a magnifying glass and opened the book to the rain forest and saw her own sandal footprints. Now she realized that it was not a dream. She was really there.

I've got to go back. I've got to go back. Maybe that is where Lezah must be and cannot get back. I've finally found a piece of evidence.

Zora had no idea at this point of how she was going to get back into the rain forest other than reading a passage from the book.

> *"Here you can wipe your tears away," said the girl as she reached in back of her head and untied her kente cloth scarf. "You see," she said, "my scarf has many colors: black for maturation that intensified spiritual energy; maroon, the color of Mother Earth associated with healing; blue for peaceful harmony, and love; green for the vegetation, planting, harvesting, growth, and spiritual renewal; and gold for the royalty, wealth, high status, glory, spiritual and purity." Her scarf was used to hold back her beautiful, kinky, soft locks of hair. The girl gave the butterfly her beautiful scarf so that her tears could prove to become a part of her family if nothing else. Since birth this little girl has always wore kente cloth fabrics, as it representing her people of color. As the butterfly quieted down, she began to tell the water lily her story. With her soft voice, she begins by describing the war between the kaleidoscope: insects, butterflies, moths, and other creatures of the air great and small. How she got turned around, and before she knew it, she got lost and in way over her head. That was how she landed in Hazel's pond. "I wished," said the butterfly to the water lily "that I could be a child instead of a butterfly.*

Having strong legs and feet would allow me to have a much better chance to find help and not land in your pond." "I would love to laugh, run, play and learn. And what I really want is to have an education." "Becoming human has always been my ultimate secret wish."

Zora was beginning to realize that this story was so real. As she dozed off, in a whisper she could hear Lezah's name being called out. In light of it all, the voice she heard was Maya calling out to Lezah to come inside the cave. She was so tired and fell into a deep sleep as she transported to the rain forest.

Meanwhile, back in the forest, some days went by. Many leaders of the metropolis of Neferzion must come together with the others to discuss the positions of the orbs.

The head leaders vowed to grow in strength in order to eradicate the raw and negative values of the lost city of Xenotopia. This city was tarnished under Jubu's rules. The focus was on the great city of Butari, which housed the orb in the largest tower in the city.

For many years this was the true energy source for the life of many planets. The leaders took great pride in knowing that the life orbs were safe in Butari. As of now there was much to be said about where this war would take place.

Everyone was prepared to fight for the safety and well-being of the main jewel that was their source of life's energy.

Orbs were round in shape, and their glow of light shines with many colors. This created the volume of higher or lower importance in how the orb could be represented in the value of life restoration.

Each city and planet had their very own source of light, as the strength of the orbs varied according to the amount of potency that was needed to be added to their life sources.

When a city was built, the realistic belief was that it was built upon a life source, which was the orbs, allowing the city to manifest greater strength. Much fear and devastation were about to take place, and many were pressed to try and understand the reasoning of this war.

Later on that night, a stillness settled all around the city of Butari and a swarm of all kinds of insects filtered. The locusts were fuming among the trees and settling their aim, lurking as they waited to take on any living object that made a movement of any kind.

Everyone took their place, for the battle was about to take place in Butari. Hazel made it very clear that everyone needed to stay inside their dwelling in the rain forest. While the army of bald eagles were heading toward Butari, the gifted were among the warriors taking their places as well.

Lezah, Maya, Zephaniah, and the others hid inside the cave where they would be safe.

13

CONQUER TO WIN

They watched now as Hazel transformed herself into Unee, dressed as a gifted warrior ready to fight. She made a public and typically formal declaration: "I will be on the battlefield. I will not be here to protect you. I have been trained as a warrior along with my other gifts." She assured them to watch out and take good care of each other.

Hazel then said, "I will be back, and upon my return, we will be entering into the new city of Quantazaire." "We will win and conquer a new life for our cities, and the population and the rights of all will be protected and tightly secured."

Hazel was aware that there was no way in or out of Waterfall Bay, so she used her powers. She then transported herself into the town of Butari where war had begun, and darkness had already filled the skies as the ammunition was heard all over.

She now positioned herself to oversee the tower. As she looked up at the tower, she could see the orb filled with lights brighter than the sun.

Who but Themba's team of bald eagles were there as guardians taking watch over the towers?

Unee then found herself overshadowed by Jubu's men as she battled her way through all the ammunition. Out of nowhere she caught a glimpse of Jubu's appearance. He was not human. He was shape-shifting as he fought. Frightening as it was, Unee continued her quest as her fight was about the orb's stability. Jubu had taken on the likeness of a horrible creature she had never seen before. How could this thing be the father of her son, Zion? Not allowing herself to be distracted, she continued to fight.

So, further into battle, she found her way to annihilate those creatures of destruction, using her weapons to annihilate her opponents who were trying to seize the orbs. She wouldn't allow herself to be defeated. Another day passed, with some losses to say the least. Jubu's army was gradually diminishing in size and losing their source of strength, while Avaszion, Neferzion, and Butari were still holding strong.

Xenotopia was weakening so much that the population there had become less than a city, as the population had moved onto other areas.

Jubu confronted Unee in the middle of all the uprising, saying, "So, you are the mother of my son. Where is my son, and what name have you placed upon him?"

Unee began to go in and out as she shape-shifted in turning herself into Hazel then Unee as Jubu followed, trying to create a personal battle amid the war that he created.

Unee would not be defeated, so she continued to fight. Now, it became her fight with Jubu. He could not be allowed to think that Zion would depart with him to the fallen city of Xenotopia, which was almost no more. They both began to teleport and shape-shift as another means or outlet made to get away. Unee made it through, and was back in the rain forest, but it became difficult for Jubu to maintain a sense of calmness as his anger had embellished his entire existence. And while thriving on an unconscious spirit, the body and mind lost focus, and the transition became difficult to perform.

Unee suddenly found her way back into Waterfall Bay, but continued to battle within herself, thinking that she was still fighting Jubu.

She saw a stranger coming out of the cave from a distance, and she tried to focus on the dark outline of something visible that was not a child or an animal.

So, as she proceeded to walk in the direction of the silhouette, out of nowhere a dark cloud of dust alerted her that something was wrong. That's when Jubu appeared. He transported himself into the rain forest not knowing that he was in Waterfall Bay he had never seen a more beautiful paradise right before his eyes.

Immediately, Waterfall Bay began deteriorating right before Unee's eyes. As she got closer to the cave, the shadow disappeared into darkness. The sun left its position and expired. There was no light, and their resources were no more. The palm trees were dying out, the waterfalls were drying up, and the vegetation was rotting away, all because of Jubu's existence in the rain forest.

It wasn't enough for Jubu to fight to take the orbs. He was now dealing with a personal vendetta to seize his son

Zion, destroy Unee, and take away her powers of many gifts to inherit his son.

GLOSSARY

Adonis (Adon-is): Maya's brother

Amazonika (**Ama**-zon-i-ka): The entire rain forest

Avaszion (A-vas-zion): Birthplace of Maya and family

Bensarru (Ben-sar-rue): Elias's dad

Butari (Bu-tar-ri): A prosperous city meaning beautiful city

Cinque (Sink): Commander general

Codlebra (Cod-lee-bra): Dace fish

Elias (Eli-as): Boy found in the rain forest and raised by Hazel

Hazel (Haz-el): A giant water lily

Hymesee (Hi-me-see): An egret that looks like white duck on stilts

Jubu (Ju-boo): Ruler of Xenotopia who also wants to control Earth a.k.a. the real world

Lenefe (Len-elf-e): Elias's mother

Lezah Hany (Lez-ah han-e): Little girl; Zora's daughter, Hazel's granddaughter

Maya (My-ya): The big butterfly

Maya's Parents names: Mother (Ada-eze): Meaning king's daughter, Father (Adeola): meaning Crown of high estate

Neferzion (Nefer-zion) the capital city of Quantazaire

Orbs: Precious stones that glow and are used for energy to give life

Quantazaire (Quan-ta-zi-air): A new city being built

Sammobia (Sam-moe-be-a): Female dragonfly

Themba (Them-bay): Female African bald eagle

Tryrome (Try-rome): Rattlesnake

Unee (U-nee): Hazel's name in human form

Waterfall Bay: Rain forest named by Hazel

Xenotopia (Zen-no-tou-pia): Entire planet ruled by Jubu

Zengorra (Zen-gor-rah): Planet taking control

Zephaniah (Zepfan-nigh-a): Baby panther

Zion (Zi-on): A place on which strength is built; Hazel's son, Lezah's uncle, and Zora's lost brother

Zora Hany (Zor-a Han-e): Lezah's mother, Hazel's daughter

CLOSING THOUGHTS

How we elevate in life can be a challenge especially when we take to much for granted in light of thinking we know everything. Sometimes working together allows us to collect a more exciting brain power to create those positive images.

Our brain can become the masterpiece for what we claim, however, have the common sense to label and market what is yours as well as having shared fame. Follow your dreams and take time to master the good in everything you set out to accomplish as your best.

Find a mean by way of making your dreams better as you see others who have made a path for you to allow their light to shine as well. There is more than enough praise set aside for everyone who values to achieve the desired aim in becoming someone famous.

Know that by example only, can those possibilities shine light on everyone to say that they are capable of becoming or doing something greater.

Not so much for praise or honor but for respect as a person in the way you embraces the love of yourself and those who have come before you.

Allow yourself to love others who may look or be different in their thoughts and ideals. Let this be the strong rule to loving all people.

Manifest love for all and conquer the ugliness that may fill your heart in those times you feel you are left behind in your talent. Develop a means to let go of the bad that surrounds your spirit and always keep in mind first and foremost to do the right things by all means necessary in life.

Reality is real, as you travel throughout life learn to stay focus on the direction of self-preservation. As a beginning for others who wish to lean in to follow the notion to test the waters, and succeed in their own right. For their accomplishments to strive to be great or the best at what they set out to do.

And lastly, what life gives us, is the right to balance our lives to love, live, and share laughter ….